Seeds! Seeds! Seeds!

Written and Illustrated by
Nancy Elizabeth Wallace

Marshall Cavendish Children

Marshall Cavendish, 99 White Plains Road, Tarrytown, NY 10591
www.marshallcavendish.us

Library of Congress Cataloging-in-Publication Data
Wallace, Nancy Elizabeth.
Seeds! Seeds! Seeds! / written and illustrated by Nancy Elizabeth Wallace.— 1st ed.
p. cm.
"Marshall Cavendish."
Summary: Buddy Bear learns about different kinds of seeds and their uses when he opens a package sent by his grandfather.
ISBN-13: 978-0-7614-5366-6 (paperback)
ISBN-10: 0-7614-5159-5 (hardcover)
[1. Seeds—Fiction. 2. Grandfathers—Fiction. 3. Bears—Fiction.] I. Title.
PZ7.W15875Se 2004
[E]—dc21
2003009318

Thanks to the Connecticut Agricultural Experiment Station
for acting as an invaluable resource.

The text of this book is set in Nobel.
The illustrations are rendered in cut paper.
Buddy's hand lettering by Lizette Boehling.
Book design by Virginia Pope.
Printed in Malaysia
First Marshall Cavendish paperback edition, 2007
1 2 3 4 5 6

March

S	M	T	W	T	F	S
			1✗	2✗	3✗	4✗
5✗	6	7	8	9	10	11
12	13	14	15	16	17	18
19	20	21	22	23	24	25
26	27	28	29	30	31	

For Carol and Ken,
Sylvia and Bill,
Doris, Phil, Clarice, Joe,
Feenie and Zeke
—great neighbors;

and unending thanks to
John Himmelman,
Martha Link Walsh,
George Nicholson, and
Alice Miller Bregman,
who helped me
plant the seed

With love,
—N. E. W.

One Monday in early March, Jim the mailman called out, "Package for Buddy Bear!"
"For me?" asked Buddy.
Jim read, "It says, 'For Buddy from Gramps.'"

Gramps
4321 Golden Springs
Coral Park, FL 33072

Buddy
8 Bluebird Lane
Mountain Hollow, ME
04211

For Buddy
from Gramps

Buddy carried the big box into the kitchen.

Mama helped him open it.

Inside were bags, tagged and tied with blue string.

Buddy lined them up.

He counted, "One . . . two . . . three . . . four . . . five."

There was a note from Gramps.

Dear Buddy,

Have five days
of fun!
Love,
Gramps

P.S. It's almost spring!

Buddy picked a bag.
What's inside? he wondered.
He and Mama read the tag:

Different and the same,
  different and the same,
Count them, sort them,
  glue them by their name.

Buddy opened the bag. Inside he found glue, markers, a piece of sturdy paper, and a small white bag.

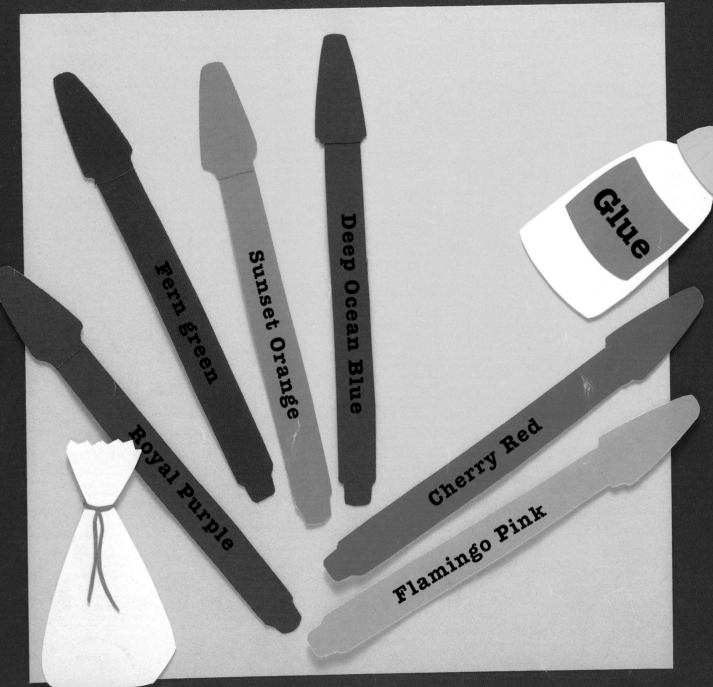

Fern green

Sunset Orange

Deep Ocean Blue

Glue

Royal Purple

Cherry Red

Flamingo Pink

Buddy shook the little bag.
It made a *shhhh-shhhh-shhhh* sound.

He peeked inside.

Then he tipped the bag.

"Seeds?" asked Buddy.
"Seeds," said Mama.
Buddy counted them.
"One, two, three, four, five, six, seven, eight, nine, ten, eleven, twelve."

He touched them.
"They feel really
hard and dry."
Mama said, "That's the
seed coat."
"The seeds have coats?"
asked Buddy.
"Yes, Bud. The hard
seed coat protects the tiny
plant curled up inside."

"Look!" said Buddy.
"What do you see?"
Mama asked.

"The seeds are different colors.
They are different shapes.
They are different sizes!
Mama, do big seeds always grow
big plants?"

"Sometimes, but not always.
Some small seeds grow into
big trees."

Buddy's Seed Collection

corn  *pea*   *radish*   *pumpkin*

Buddy sorted the seeds.

"I see seeds that look like corn and seeds that look like peas."

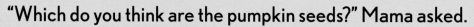

"Which do you think are the pumpkin seeds?" Mama asked.

"The big ones," said Buddy. "I remember them from when

I carved my jack-o'-lantern. I think the littlest ones must be radish seeds."

"I think you are very smart," said Mama.

Then Buddy glued the seeds next to their names.

"Corn, pea, radish, pumpkin. I'm hungry. Let's eat!"

Mama and Buddy had a snack.
"Seeds, seeds, seeds!" said Buddy.

He saved some apple seeds for his collection.

Buddy's Seed Collection

corn

pea

radish

pumpkin

Apple

On Tuesday, Buddy lined up the bags. He closed his eyes and pointed.

Mama and Buddy read the tag:

Look, look, look!
How do I grow?
Put me in order,
Then you will know.

Buddy opened the bag.

"Gramps made cards. I like cards!" said Buddy.

"The cards show how a seed germinates," said Mama.

Buddy giggled. "Germinates! Does that mean it has germs?"

Mama giggled too. "Noooo, *germinate* means
to start to grow!"

"Why do seeds start to grow?" asked Buddy.

Mama explained, "To start growing, seeds need oxygen from the air, the right temperature, and water. A seed soaks up the water. The water softens the seed coat and makes it swell. The seed coat splits open, and the seed begins to grow."

Buddy put the cards in order. "How does a seed know what to grow?"

"Each seed grows the same kind of plant that it came from," said Mama.

"Inside each seed is the beginning of a tiny plant called the embryonic plant."

"Em-bree-on-ick," said Buddy.

seed

root

"Yes, Bud. The tiny plant has a tiny embryonic root,

leaves

stem

food

a tiny embryonic stem,

tiny embryonic leaves,

and food to nourish the tiny plant as it starts to grow."

"Food!" said Buddy. "I'm hungry. Let's eat."

Buddy and Mama had a snack.
"Seeds, seeds, SEEDS!" said Buddy.

He saved some cantaloupe and watermelon seeds
for his collection.

Buddy's Seed Collection

corn

pea

radish

pumpkin

Watermelon

Apple

cantaloupe

When Wednesday came, Buddy said, "Another day, another bag."

He and Mama read:

Here is something you can eat,
For the birds it is a treat.
Just for them and just for you,
Good nutrition, energy too.

"Something to eat. I like this bag already," said Buddy.

Buddy looked inside. He found a small bird feeder with a red roof. There were also two clear bags with seeds.

For the birds—
sunflower seeds

For my buddy Buddy—
sunflower seeds

"Mine look different," said Buddy.

"The seeds for the birds still have their hard coats," said Mama. "The seeds for you have had their hard coats taken off and their insides toasted. That makes them good to eat!"

"Good to eat! I'll have one right now," said Buddy. He popped one in his mouth.

Then he filled the feeder with the bird seeds. He saved some for his collection.

Buddy and Mama went outside. Buddy pressed the suction cups against the glass. The little bird feeder stuck to the window.

When they went back inside, Buddy asked,
"Will these seeds grow inside of me?"
"No, Buddy. They won't grow inside of you. But the
seeds we eat are good food full of vitamins and minerals.
Your morning cereal is made from the seeds of wheat,
oats, rice, and corn."

Mama tasted Buddy's sunflower seeds. "They taste nutty," she said.
"And yummy!" said Buddy.

He saved one toasted sunflower seed for his collection.

Buddy's Seed Collection

corn

pea

radish

pumpkin

Watermelon

Apple

sunflower seed without a coat

sunflower seeds with coats

cantaloupe

On Thursday, Buddy said, "This one today."

Cub Camp

Mama and Buddy read the tag:

Glue these on,
Make a nice design.
Create a picture frame
That is mighty fine.

Buddy emptied the bag.

"Look what Gramps sent you in this one," said Mama.

"Different bean seeds, a cardboard frame, and more glue!"

"I like gluing seeds!" said Buddy.

Later Buddy and Mama had a snack.
"Strawberries!" Buddy said. "I see teeny-tiny seeds."

Mama said, "And strawberries are the only fruit
with seeds on the—"
"Outside!" shouted Buddy.

Buddy added some bean seeds
and some tiny strawberry seeds to his collection.

Buddy's Seed Collection

corn

pea

radish

pumpkin

watermelon

apple

sunflower seed
without a coat

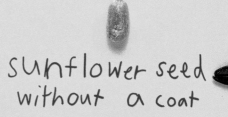

sunflower seeds
with coats

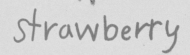

strawberry

cantaloupe

beans

When Friday came, Buddy chuckled. "Which one
should I pick today? I think I'll pick this one."
He and Mama read:

Here are some things you can sow.
Water them, watch them
   sprout and grow.
Though it takes a little while,
Surely this will make you smile.

Gramps had put the bottom half of a plastic bottle,
some potting soil, grass seed, tape, and
paper shapes in the bag. Buddy knew just what to do.

He poured the soil into the bottle.

He sprinkled the seeds over the top
and covered them with a little soil.

Next he watered the seeds.

Then he taped the paper shapes to the bottle.
"Now I'm really hungry!" said Buddy.

He and Mama had a snack.

Buddy saved some pear seeds for his collection.

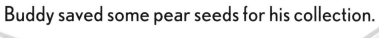

Buddy's Seed Collection

corn

pea

radish

pumpkin

watermelon

apple

sunflower seed without a coat

sunflower seeds with coats

pear

strawberry

cantaloupe

beans

For several days Buddy watched.

He watered . . .

and waited.

While he waited, Buddy read some books.
He brought his seed collection to school.
He rode his bike and played catch with Dad.

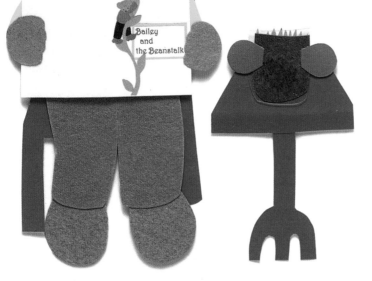

He built a model airplane at Cub Club
and went to his best friend Albert's birthday party.

After a while...

Buddy sent a package to Gramps.

Mary

Buddy
Gramps
131 Golden Springs
Coral Park, FL 32072

Dear Gramps,
seeds, seeds, seeds
are so much fun!
Thank you lots
from your grandson.
LoVe, Buddy